The Family Book

TODD PARR

LB

LITTLE, BROWN AND COMPANY
New York Boston

ABDO
Spotlight

ABDOBOOKS.COM

Reinforced library bound edition published in 2020 by Spotlight, a division of ABDO, PO Box 398166, Minneapolis, Minnesota 55439. Spotlight produces high-quality reinforced library bound editions for schools and libraries. Published by agreement with Little, Brown and Company.

Printed in the United States of America, North Mankato, Minnesota.
042019
092019

THIS BOOK CONTAINS
RECYCLED MATERIALS

LB LITTLE, BROWN

Hachette Book Group
237 Park Avenue, New York, NY 10017

Little, Brown and Company is a division of Hachette Book Group, Inc.
The Little, Brown name and logo are trademarks of Hachette Book Group, Inc.

First Paperback Edition: May 2010
Originally published in hardcover in October 2003 by Little, Brown and Company

Library of Congress Control Number: 2019930051

Publisher's Cataloging-in-Publication Data

Names: Parr, Todd, author. | Parr, Todd, illustrator.
Title: The family book / by Todd Parr; illustrated by Todd Parr.
Description: Minneapolis, Minnesota : Spotlight, 2020. | Series: Todd Parr picture books
Summary: This title features a variety of families from big and small, to some with only one parent or some with two moms and dads - but all alike in some ways and special no matter what.
Identifiers: ISBN 9781532143700 (lib. bdg.)
Subjects: LCSH: Families--Juvenile fiction. | Family relationships--Juvenile fiction. | Children of divorced parents--Juvenile fiction. | Single-parent families--Juvenile fiction.
Classification: DDC [E]--dc23

ABDO

Spotlight

A Division of ABDO
abdobooks.com

To my family—who sometimes
did not understand me,
but encouraged me to
go after everything I wanted
even when we did not agree.
As I now realize—this takes
a lot of love to do.

—T. P.

Some families are big

Some families are small

Some families are the same color

Some families are different colors

All families
Like to
HUG each
Other!

Some families live near each other

Some families live far from each other

Some families look alike

Some families look like their pets

All families are Sad when they lose someone they Love.

Some families have a stepmom or stepdad and stepsisters or stepbrothers

Some families adopt children

Some families have two
moms or two dads

Some families have one parent instead of two

All families like to celebrate special days together!

Some families eat the same things

Some families eat different things

Some families like to be quiet

Some families like to be clean

Some families like to be messy

Some families live in a house by themselves

Some families share a house with other families

All families
each other

can help

be STRONG!

There are lots of different ways to be a family.  Your family is special no matter what kind it is.

♥ Love, Todd